# the
# House
# of
# Clouds

# The House of Clouds

Lisa Thompson

With illustrations by
Alice McKinley

Barrington Stoke

First published in 2020 in Great Britain by
Barrington Stoke Ltd
18 Walker Street, Edinburgh, EH3 7LP

www.barringtonstoke.co.uk

Text © 2020 Lisa Thompson
Illustrations © 2020 Alice McKinley

A CIP catalogue record for this book is available
from the British Library upon request

ISBN: 978-1-78112-906-7

Printed by Hussar Books, Poland

*To Paul and Nick*

# Chapter 1

Grandad's dog, Buster, was so embarrassing. He was a small, scruffy terrier, and he barked at *everything*. He also smelt of damp old socks, which made our house smell too.

Grandad and Buster came to live with us a few months ago. The doggy smell was always the first thing I noticed when I got home from school. Then one day I noticed something else as well. An ugly white rail had appeared on the wall beside our front door.

"Don't forget Buster's walk, Tabitha!" Grandad shouted as soon as I walked in. I huffed and dropped my school bag down by the bottom of the stairs.

"Yes, Grandad!" I yelled back. "And it's Tabby, not Tabitha," I said under my breath.

Mum appeared from Grandad's room carrying a tray. "Hello, love," she said to me. "Everything OK?"

"What's that thing by the front door, Mum?" I asked. "It looks awful!"

"It's to help your grandad get up and down the step," Mum said. "We can't risk him having another fall."

"But Grandad doesn't go anywhere!" I snapped. "He just sits in his room and looks at his maps all day." *And takes up space in our house*, I thought. But I didn't say that bit out loud.

Mum and Dad had converted our dining room into a bedroom for Grandad. They put his bed exactly where our dining table used to be. At dinner time we had to cram around a tiny table in the kitchen. Grandad ate his meal in an armchair, from a tray on his lap.

"For a start," said Mum, "the rail will help me get him to the car when I take him to his appointments."

A glossy leaflet for walk-in baths lay on the hall table. On the front was an old lady wearing a pink dressing gown. My stomach sank.

"We're not getting one of those baths, are we?!" I said.

Mum rubbed her forehead.

"I don't know yet," she said. "Try to be a bit more considerate, Tabby. Things are hard enough as it is."

Everything changed when Grandad came to live with us. Mum had to give up her job at the doctor's surgery so that she could look after him. Then weird things began appearing around the house.  First it was a grey walking frame that stood beside the fridge and got in everybody's way.  Then a horrible padded seat was fixed onto our downstairs toilet.  Dad said it was so that Grandad could be as independent as possible, but he still didn't seem able to do anything on his own.  Mum always had to help Grandad, and she didn't have time for anyone else.

"Tabitha?  Are you there?" Grandad called. "Buster is waiting for his walk."

"Coming, Grandad," I moaned back.  Mum gave me a stern look as she went to the kitchen. It was my job to take Grandad's stinky dog for a walk each day after school, and I hated it.  I went into Grandad's room.

"Ah!  There you are!" said Grandad, smiling. He had one of his maps spread out over his lap. "I would love to see Japan one day, wouldn't you?"  Grandad tapped his finger on the map. "I hear they have the most wonderful cherry

blossom in the spring.  What a sight that
would be."

I shrugged.  "I guess," I said.  Buster waddled
over towards me, his tail wagging.  He knew
that when I got home it meant walkies-time.

"I think I'll put that on my list," said
Grandad, picking up a notebook that he kept
beside him.

I watched as Grandad wrote *Japan* in shaky writing. There were ten places on the list, including *Alaska* and *The Isle of Bute*. These were all places Grandad wanted to visit one day. But I didn't think it was likely, considering he found it difficult to get to the bathroom. Grandad hadn't travelled at all, apart from a few holidays in Spain with my nana, who died long before I was born. He'd been on his own ever since.

I turned to go, but Grandad started talking again.

"Have I ever told you about my ship in a bottle?" he said.

Grandad always did this: he told me to take Buster for a walk, but he wanted to chat at the same time.

"Yes, Grandad," I said. He'd told me about his ship in a bottle at least a hundred times.

"That ship was made by some very skilled craftsmen," said Grandad, ignoring what I'd just said. His eyes twinkled as he got ready to explain the twist in the tale.

"Did you know that—" Grandad began.

"It was made by specially trained bumble bees?" I interrupted him, rolling my eyes. "Yes, Grandad. You've already told me. Many times."

Grandad's ridiculous stories got on my nerves, but he just grinned and clapped his hands together.

"That's right!" he said. "The pieces of the ship were placed inside the glass bottle, and then the bees set to work with their tiny hammers and nails. They were so small they could fit inside, you see? It's a marvellous thing, don't you think?"

I glanced at the old ship in a bottle standing at the front of a shelf. The glass of the bottle was tinted green, and inside was a little wooden ship, complete with rigging and sails. It was very clever, and I had no idea how the ship had been pushed inside the narrow neck. But I knew it definitely hadn't been made by bees.

I sighed. Grandad seemed to think I was six, not twelve.

"I'd better get going, Grandad," I said.

I went to the hallway and took Buster's lead off the hook by the front door. He quickly trotted after me. As I clipped the lead onto his collar, he brushed against my hand, and I wiped it on my school trousers. Buster's fur was disgusting. It was really greasy, with scaly flakes stuck in it. Mum kept saying she'd take him to the vets, but she'd been so busy with Grandad she hadn't had a chance.

"Come on then, Stink," I said to the dog. "Let's get this over with." I opened the front door, and we headed down to the beach.

# Chapter 2

I planned to take my normal route: down to
the pier, turn left past the beach huts, on to the
shingle beach (that allows dogs), up the steps,
over the field, across the car park and home.
I could do the whole loop in about twenty-five
minutes if Buster didn't keep stopping.

We turned right at the end of my road, and
I stopped. On the pavement in front of us was a
blue wheelie bin.

"Oh no," I groaned.

Buster spotted it and began to yap very
loudly. For some unknown reason, Buster got
very angry with blue wheelie bins. Every time

he barked, his feet left the ground.  He looked just like a plastic wind-up dog toy I had when I was small.

"Shut up, Buster!" I said as I pulled on his lead.

He crouched down low, dug his paws into the pavement and did a deep growl.  Then he started jumping and barking again.  A curtain twitched, and a woman looked out of her window.

"Buster, I said be quiet!" I yelled again, tugging on his lead.

"You shouldn't pull your dog like that," a voice said.

I looked across the road.  It was Alex Walters from my form.  I ignored him.  Alex was a bit of a weirdo.  With any luck he'd just go away.

I turned and tried to drag Buster back towards home. He wasn't going to go for a walk at all if he was going to behave like this. But Buster strained against the lead and wouldn't budge. He was surprisingly strong for a small dog.

"Just yanking his lead isn't going to help," said Alex, appearing beside me. "What you've got to remember is that dogs bark for a reason."

I could barely hear Alex above Buster's noise.

"Figure out *why* he's barking, *then* you can work on a solution to stop him," said Alex.

Buster had gone back to deep growling now. I guessed he was beginning to wear himself out.

"He's barking because he's an idiot," I said.

Alex blinked at me. I thought he was a bit shocked I could talk about an animal like that, but I didn't care.

"I don't think he is an idiot," said Alex. He crouched down and tickled Buster on the head. "Are you, boy?"

Buster instantly stopped growling and spun around, licking Alex's hand.

"See?" Alex said. "He just wanted a head rub, didn't you, little fella?"

Buster's eyes went all droopy as Alex tickled him around his ears.

"But you might want to take him to the vet," Alex went on. "I think he might have some kind of skin condition."

"Right, well, thanks for your help," I said, checking the road. "Come on, Buster, let's go." I quickly crossed the street with Buster trotting beside me, leaving Alex behind.

When we got to the pier, Buster stopped to lick up an ice cream that had been dropped beside one of those "grab a soft toy" machines. As I waited, I stared at the mound of stuffed fluffy frogs behind the glass. They'd been crammed in so tightly, the chances of picking one up with the silver claw seemed pretty unlikely.

"Sugar isn't good for dogs, you know," a familiar voice called out. It was Alex again.

He must have followed me. The ice cream had all gone and Buster was now licking the pavement.

"At least he's cleaning up the mess," I said.

Alex smiled.

There was a scream and laughter coming from the sandy beach down on the right of the pier. We both looked over, and I spotted a crowd of kids from our year. They went to the beach most days after school. Rebecca Hayes was running to the water's edge. The sea splashed up her legs, and she let out a squeal. It was early November, so it must have been freezing. Lily Carter was sitting on the sand, weaving her hair into a plait.

Rebecca and I used to be really good friends, but last summer her family had gone on holiday with Lily's family. They'd been inseparable ever since. Apparently, Rebecca and Lily were going to France together for Christmas as well. That

would never happen with my family.  Not now
we'd got Grandad and a stupid dog to look after.

Alex was tickling Buster's ears again.

"It looks like some kind of dermatitis
that he's got," Alex said.  "I think we've got a
medicated shampoo at home that would help."

Buster sat down and pressed himself against
Alex's leg.  Alex tickled him under his armpit.
Buster pressed against my leg sometimes, but I
never stroked him.

"How do you know so much about dogs?"
I said.

"My mum's a vet," said Alex.  "I want to be a
vet too one day.  Did you know it takes longer to
train to be a vet than it does to be a doctor?"

I shook my head.

"Doctors learn about the human body," Alex went on, "but vets have to learn about a variety of animals. A cat is going to need different care to a hamster. It makes sense when you think about it."

It did make sense, but I didn't say anything.

The screaming and shouting from the beach got louder. Alex gazed over at the group. I wasn't sure who his friends were. I always saw him on his own.

"Animals are a lot easier to deal with than human beings, don't you think?" Alex said.

I just shrugged. I was worried that Rebecca or Lily might spot me, so I decided to keep walking.

"I'd better get going," I said.

Alex quickly ruffled the top of Buster's head.

"I'll find some of that dog shampoo if you like?" he said. "I don't mind helping you bath him."

"Yeah, maybe," I said. But there was no way I was going to give Buster a bath.

I pulled Buster away, and he trotted beside me as we headed towards the beach huts.

# Chapter 3

I let Buster off his lead, and he ran down onto
the beach as I walked along the promenade.
He never went near the sea, but he had a good
sniff around the pebbles.  As I walked, I read the
names of the beach huts, even though I'd read
them a thousand times before.

"Surf Shack, Beach Nut, Mary's Place, Ship
Shape," I said out loud.  Some of the names were
supposed to be funny, but they didn't make me
laugh.  "Little Crab, Ahoy There, Vitamin Sea."

The huts were painted in different pastel
shades, and each name sign was nailed to the
peak of the roof.  Some people had even painted
little pictures on the signs, like a deckchair or

a fish. I stopped at a hut called "Carter's Crazy Cabin", which belonged to Lily's family. I peered into the window.

Along one side was a sky-blue bench with a white padded seat. At the back of the hut was a table with a camp stove, a kettle and an assortment of cups and plates. Hanging around the walls were strings of pink and white bunting. Everything you'd need for a day at the beach was stacked in the corner: folding chairs, beach towels, a kite, a deflated rubber boat and some bats and balls. Last summer, Rebecca and Lily had posted loads of photos of themselves at the beach hut. It had felt like they'd been there every single week.

Buster began yapping at the waves. He ran back and forth, his tail wagging as he barked. He was such an idiot. I got to the end of the beach huts and called him.

"Buster! Come on! Come up here!"

The little dog scampered across the pebbles and up the wooden steps to meet me. When he got to the top, he stopped and let me clip on his lead before we carried on.

The further we walked, the more rough and rocky the beach became. The pebbles turned into large boulders, and there were no more pretty beach huts. No one really came to this end of the beach, only fishermen and the occasional jogger. Up on the headland was a single house that faced out to the grey sea. It had been abandoned for years, and its dark windows looked like blank unseeing eyes.

Buster and I turned left into the field that led to a car park. As we walked, we went past a dirt track that led to the empty clifftop house on the headland. Buster knew our route and pulled me towards the car park, but I stopped.

"Hang on a minute, Buster," I said. "Let's go and take a look at the house, shall we?"

I'd never walked up the path before, and I don't know why I suddenly decided to do it then. I wasn't even sure if I'd be trespassing.

"Come on, we won't be long," I said, and I walked along the dirt track with Buster plodding beside me.

# Chapter 4

At the end of the track was a wall of long grass
and weeds. I stopped and stared at the house.
It was much larger than it looked from the
beach, and it had two pale green turrets on the
roof. A rusty weather vane spun in the wind
on one of the turrets. The only weather vanes
I had seen before had a chicken or a cockerel
in the middle, but this one had the shape of the
sun peeking out from behind a cloud.

Buster sat down beside me and began to
whine.

"Let's take a closer look," I said. "Just five
more minutes."

As we walked towards the house, the weeds
scratched against my legs, and Buster vanished.
I only knew he was still there because his
movements swayed the long grass beside me.

We emerged at the front of the house, and
Buster gave himself a good shake. A bundle

of post was poking out of the letterbox, and I relaxed a bit. If anyone was home, surely they would have taken the mail in?

I looked up. The brickwork of the house had once been painted white, but it was peeling off and underneath I could see dark grey plaster.

"Let's take a look around the side," I said to Buster. He couldn't understand me, but talking to him made me feel less nervous.

At the side of the house was an old car missing two front wheels, with a big dent in the bonnet. Beside the car was a barn. It was made of black corrugated sheets of metal, and out of one side came a large shiny silver funnel that curled and pointed up into the sky.

"What's that?" I said, staring up at the funnel. "It looks like a giant trumpet." The barn had two wide doors at the end, and beside them was a small circular window.

"I'm going to take a look inside," I said to Buster.

The window was covered with a thick film of dirt, so I used the sleeve of my jumper to clean a small patch to look through. I blinked into the gloom. In the centre of the barn was a large shape covered with grey sheeting. Ropes snaked out from beneath the sheeting, tied to silver hoops that were cemented to the ground. Large faded sheets of paper were pinned to one wall, covered in complicated diagrams. Below them was a desk scattered with pens, papers, binoculars and a few objects I didn't recognise. Beside the desk was a shelving unit stuffed with cardboard boxes. I could just make out some of the words printed on the front of the boxes: rain gauge, anemometer, thermometers.

A glass cabinet stood beside the large, bulging shape under the sheeting. Something glinted behind the cabinet doors. At first I thought it was silver cups or maybe trophies. But then I realised exactly what was inside.

On each of the three shelves were dozens of knives, propped up as if they were on display in a museum.

They were not the kind of knives that you would use to eat your dinner, but sharp gleaming daggers. Some of the knives had ornate swirls and patterns carved into their shiny blades and some had twisted wooden handles. There were large ones like swords and smaller ones the size of my palm. All of them looked incredibly sharp.

I was just about to clean another area of the window when the grey sheeting caught my eye. It was moving! It rose and fell as if there was a large creature trapped underneath. My heart raced. Whatever it was under there, I really didn't want it to see me.

"Come on, Buster! RUN!" I said as we raced away towards the long grass.

We ran through the weeds, past the house and down the dirt track. When we got to the end, Buster stopped and wouldn't run any further. I looked back, expecting something to be chasing us, but there was nothing there.

There was just the house surrounded by the long swaying grass. It must have been a draught or something that had made the sheet move.

"Aren't I silly?" I said to Buster. He looked up at me, panting. "Fancy getting scared because of the wind?"

At the end of the track was a square wooden sign lying face down on the ground. I lifted it up and read:

**The House of Clouds**

# Chapter 5

By the time we got across the car park, Buster was tired and refused to walk any further. He sat on his bottom and wouldn't budge.

"Come on," I said. "I want to get home, not hang around here with a stinky dog." I also wanted to get away from the creepy house.

Buster took a deep breath, then lay down, putting his head on his front paws. I sighed. There was nothing else for it. I'd have to carry him.

"You do realise that you smell really, really badly, don't you?" I said as I picked Buster up.

His little tail wagged under my armpit. He was such a stupid dog. But as I walked I began to enjoy the feeling of Buster's warm body against my chest. It was getting cold, and the strange barn had made me feel even more chilled.

When we got to our street, the bright white rail by our door stood out more than ever. I sighed, put Buster down on the ground and used my keys to get in.

"Is that you, Tabitha?" Grandad called out. "Is Buster OK? You've been gone so long."

"He's fine," I said. I unclipped Buster's lead and he trotted to Grandad's room.

"Come and tell me all about it," Grandad said. "Have they moved the beach huts yet?"

"No, they're still there," I said, hovering by the door.

Two winters ago, there had been a terrible storm. The waves had crashed in like huge claws. They'd snatched the pastel huts and pulled them out to the deep, dark sea. I imagined the colourful huts bobbing around on the murky waves, with buckets, spades and tea cups clattering around inside. From then on, the council moved all the huts back from the beach when the season began to change – into the field by the car park where the sea couldn't reach them.

"I remember me and your nana used to love that spot by the beach," Grandad said. "We'd sit there for hours and plan our travels. We felt like we had all the time in the world to visit new places."

He looked down at the map on his lap. It was a different one this time – of Australia.

"So, tell me," Grandad said, clearly wanting to chat. "Where else did you go?"

His chest rose and fell quickly. Grandad did three breaths to my one. I counted them once.

"Down to the pier, along the front and then around the back of the car park," I said. I didn't mention the house, as I wasn't sure if I should have gone there. I was itching to get to my room and check my phone. I wanted to see if Rebecca and Lily had posted any photographs from the beach. It made me feel sad when I saw them, but I couldn't stop myself from looking.

"And how is the House of Clouds looking these days?" said Grandad, folding his map. "I haven't seen that place in years."

He shuffled forwards in his seat. Buster was lying down at Grandad's feet, snoring already.

I remembered the sign lying on the track to the house on the clifftop. "Who lived there?" I asked.

"It used to belong to an artist called Ava Laurent," Grandad said. "She was a friend of your nana's. She was very skilled. Especially when it came to carving the cumulus cloud."

I had no idea what he was talking about.

"What's a cumulus cloud?" I asked.

"You know those fluffy white clouds that look a bit like candy floss?" said Grandad.

I nodded.

"Well, those are cumulus clouds. That's their scientific name, anyway. Ava Laurent always used to say those clouds were the best for carving. Nice and chunky, you see? Like a giant piece of foam. Perfect for her carving knives."

The scary knives in the cabinet! I felt goosebumps tickle down my arms. But what did Grandad mean about them being knives for carving clouds? I watched him as he sat back in his chair and picked up a cup, taking a slurp of tea. I was going to ask Grandad about the knives, but then I caught sight of the ship in a bottle up on the shelf and remembered his story about the bees. I shook my head. This stuff about carving clouds must be another one of Grandad's crazy stories. He was always saying weird stuff. Mum and Dad said to be polite to him but ignore it.

"That's really interesting, Grandad," I said. "But I'd better get on."

I turned to leave, but he carried on talking.

"Have I ever told you about Ava Laurent, Tabitha?" he said, leaning forwards.

I shook my head.

"Maybe you could tell me another time?" I said. "I've got homework to do and ..."

Grandad sat back in his seat again.

"There aren't many of them left now, you know," he said, shaking his head.

I stared at him.

"Aren't many of who left?" I said.

"Have a seat, Tabitha," Grandad said, smiling.

I sighed and slowly made my way to the dining chair beside his armchair and sat down.

"Ava Laurent was the finest cloud sculptor that this country has ever seen," Grandad began.

I snorted. "A cloud sculptor?" I said, raising my eyebrows.

Grandad nodded. "Yes, Tabitha. You know the shapes that you sometimes see in the clouds when they're floating right above you? Like a lion, perhaps, or a mermaid?"

I nodded. I'd seen one just the other week
on my way to school. It had looked like a bear
wearing a top hat.

"Well, those cloud shapes aren't accidental,
you know," Grandad said. "They are the work of
a cloud sculptor."

He leaned forwards and rested his elbows on his knees. "Ava had this marvellous contraption attached to the side of her barn that sucked clouds down from the sky. Then Ava would tie the cloud to the ground. All they want to do is float back up to the sky, you see? But when she'd finished carving one, the roof of the barn would retract, and the cloud would gently drift back up into the sky for everyone to enjoy."

I frowned. I remembered seeing that weird silver funnel sticking out of the side of the barn. And there had definitely been something moving under that sheet. Could it have been a cloud? I smirked to myself. Of course not! I was being taken in by one of Grandad's stupid stories, as if I was six years old again. When he began to talk about rubbish like this, the best thing for me to do was to make a quick exit.

"Right, well, like I said, I've got homework to be getting on with and ..."

"Do you want to see some photographs of Ava's work?" Grandad asked. He suddenly began to cough, and he patted himself on his chest a few times until it subsided. Grandad coughed a lot when he got excited about something.

"You see that box on my wardrobe?" he said. "Pass it down and I can show you what an amazing cloud artist Ava was."

I glanced up to the top of the wardrobe and spotted a small grey shoebox. It looked a bit old and battered.

"I don't have time now, Grandad," I said, standing up. "Sorry."

"Cloud sculptors won't exist at all soon," said Grandad sadly. "It seems that people don't look up any more. Too busy staring down at their phones and whatnot. It's so sad."

I put my hand into my pocket, and my fingers felt my phone. Rebecca and Lily had probably posted at least ten pictures by now.

"Sorry, Grandad," I said. "Maybe you can tell me about it another day?"

Grandad looked up at me. He seemed to be deep in thought for a moment, then he smiled and nodded.

"Of course," he said. "You get on with what you need to do, Tabitha. I can tell you all about Ava another time."

I turned away and headed upstairs, looking at my phone as I went.

# Chapter 6

Saturday passed in a blur of chores, then I spent most of Sunday in my bedroom. I read a book and checked social media to find out what Rebecca and Lily were doing. Dad popped in and asked if I'd like to go for a bike ride, but I said no.

Rebecca and Lily had got the bus into town to do some shopping. They'd bought the same pair of earrings and matching tops from the market. Rebecca had bought the top in white and Lily in black. They'd also got milkshakes and hot dogs for lunch.

I knew all this because they were constantly posting photographs. At three o'clock I threw my phone across the room and tried to read a book. My eyes followed the lines of words, but I just couldn't concentrate. I was so jealous of Rebecca and Lily I felt sick.

Mum called up to me, asking if I'd unload the dishwasher, so I trudged downstairs. I could feel Mum watching me while I was doing it.

"Is everything OK, Tabby?" she said. "You're really quiet today. We've hardly seen you."

"I'm fine," I said, avoiding Mum's eyes. "I'm just tired." I threw the cutlery into the drawer. Grandad called for Mum, so she headed to his room and I avoided any more questions.

A couple of hours later, I was lying on my bed watching some videos on my phone when I heard something going on downstairs. I went out onto the landing and saw Mum letting in two women wearing green uniforms. They looked like paramedics.

"Mum? What's going on?" I called.

Dad appeared as Mum ushered the paramedics into Grandad's room.

"Grandad's had a bit of a funny turn," Dad said.

"Is he going to be OK?" I said.

Dad pressed his lips together. "I'm sure he'll be better when we get him to hospital. Let's see what the paramedics say, shall we?"

Then Dad disappeared into Grandad's room.

I sat down at the top of the stairs for a while and listened, and then I went back to my room to see if I could hear anything through the floor. After a while, Dad came in.

"We're off to the hospital now," Dad said. "I'm going to drive, and your mum has gone in the ambulance with Grandad."

I could tell by Dad's eyes that he was worried.

"What's wrong with Grandad?" I said. "Is it serious?"

"We don't know yet," said Dad. "Don't worry. I'll text you and let you know what's going on. Can you feed Buster, please, love?"

Dad turned and I followed him out to the landing. As the front door closed behind him, the house went silent. I walked downstairs. Grandad had a lot of health problems, and he took lots of tablets each day, but I was sure he was going to be OK.

Buster appeared and sniffed at the gap below the front door. He then sat down and began to whine.

"It's OK, Buster," I said. "Grandad is just getting checked out. Shall we give you your dinner?"

When Buster heard the word "dinner", he licked his lips and followed me out to the kitchen.

I leaned against the sink and watched as Buster ate. It was quite cute how his nose pressed on his bowl as he tried to dig out the pieces from the sides. When Buster had finished, he sat down and stared at me as if to say, "And now what?"

I went upstairs and got my phone, but there were no messages. I knew that there could be a lot of waiting around in the hospital. I might not hear anything for hours yet.

I typed a text to Rebecca:

Hiya. You OK? My grandad has just gone to hospital ☹. Do you fancy coming over for a bit? We could make some cookies? Tabby x

I put my phone in my pocket and went back downstairs. There were a few mugs in the sink, so I decided to do a bit of washing up while I waited for news. Buster came over and sat down by my feet, leaning against my leg. I gently nudged him away. When I'd finished the washing up, I dried my hands and checked my phone. There was a message from Rebecca:

Tabby! That's awful! I really hope your grandad is OK. Can't come over I'm afraid. At the ice rink now. R x

I opened the social media site that Rebecca used all the time. The first photo that appeared was of Rebecca and Lily holding on to each other and laughing as they took a selfie on the ice.

I felt Buster's wiry fur against my legs again.

"Would you get away from me?" I said to Buster. "You're Grandad's dog, not mine, OK?"

I moved away and Buster slumped a bit, then he sat back up and watched me.

I made myself a cheese sandwich, then went to the lounge. I didn't fancy watching TV, but I put it on anyway. Buster followed and lay down by the sofa. He kept one eye open, watching me.

It began to get dark, and I put the lamp on and drew the curtains. I didn't like being on my own when it was dark, so I was grateful I had Buster for company, even if he did smell.

I watched a film. An hour after it had finished, I got a text:

**We're on our way home now. Hope you're OK. See you soon. Dad x**

As soon as I heard the key in the door, I went out into the hall.

"Dad? What's going on?" I said. Mum was behind him. She'd clearly been crying.

"Mum? What's happened? Where's Grandad?" I said.

Dad was frowning as he closed the door. He looked exhausted.

"I'm so sorry, Tabby," he said. "Your grandad ..." He paused as something caught in his throat. "Your grandad has passed away."

I heard what he'd said, but the words jumbled up in my head.

"What?" I said, looking between Mum and Dad.

Mum came forwards and put her arms around me.

"Grandad died, honey," she said. "I'm so sorry. He had a massive stroke while we were in the hospital. There was nothing they could do."

"But ... but you were just getting him checked over?" I said. "I thought he was going to be OK!"

I could hear my voice getting louder. How was this possible?

"He was very unwell, Tabby," said Dad. "I'm so sorry. I know it's a shock."

We stood in the hallway, all of us completely stunned. Dad pulled me and Mum into a big hug, and we stood there, holding each other. I heard Buster's claws tip-tapping as he came up to us. He sat down and leaned against my leg. This time I didn't push him away.

# Chapter 7

The next day I woke in a panic. I checked my clock and realised I was late for school. My heart pounded and I was just about to jump out of bed, and then I remembered that I didn't have to go in.

Grandad had died.

The shock of remembering what had happened was like a punch in the stomach. I couldn't believe it. Grandad was gone, and I would never see him again.

I went downstairs. Mum and Dad were busy making phone calls and letting people know what had happened. There was an old file on the kitchen table that must have been full of Grandad's paperwork.

"Are you OK, Tabby?" said Mum.

I nodded, and she gave me a quick hug.

"Can you check on Buster?" Mum asked. "He's not eaten anything this morning, and he keeps wandering around. I think he's trying to find Grandad."

I was grateful to have something to do, but it felt weird going back into Grandad's room. Mum had stripped his bed, and his slippers were still down by his armchair. On the table next to the chair were Grandad's pile of maps and his notebook with all the places he'd never get to visit. Buster was lying in his usual spot. He wagged his tail and got up to greet me.

"Hello, Stink," I said. "You don't know what's going on, do you? Poor thing."

Buster sat down and sighed. I walked over to the shelf where the ship in a bottle stood. I peered inside the bottle at the tiny wooden ship that Grandad said had been made by specially trained bumble bees. Although his made-up story used to annoy me, I wished he was here now to tell me it all over again.

I looked up at the cardboard shoebox on top of the wardrobe. Grandad had said it was full of photographs. He'd said they had something to do with the strange house on the cliff, the House of Clouds. At the time I'd been too eager to get away and back to my phone to look. I wished I'd taken more time to listen to him.

I got a chair, stood on the seat and reached up for the box. It was covered with a thin layer of dust. I got down and decided to look inside the box in my room. It felt strange being in Grandad's room when he wasn't there.

Buster followed me to the stairs.

"You stay there, Buster," I said as the little dog sat down by the bottom step. "I won't be long."

I put the shoebox on my bed and slowly removed the lid. At first I thought the pictures were ones that had gone wrong. It looked as if the photographer had dropped their camera and accidentally taken pictures of the sky. I picked up a small handful.

"Weird," I said as I turned a square photograph around in my hand. It was of a bright blue sky and some white fluffy clouds.

I picked up another photo and another, but they were all just the same: random photographs of white clouds. I was about to pile them all back into the box when I spotted something. One of the photographs was of the seafront, with the pier on one side. In the sky was a great grey and white cloud that looked exactly like a dragon. It had a long, pointed tail that swept upwards as if to escape the waves and a hooded eye that stared back at the viewer.

I turned the photograph over.  Something was written on the back:

**Dragon by Ava Laurent**
**April 1980**

I picked up another photo.  In this one the cloud looked like a peacock: it had a fan of feathers standing tall and proud behind its smooth, pointed head.  I looked on the back:

**Peacock by Ava Laurent**
**June 1977**

I raked my hand through the box, studying picture after picture.  They weren't accidental photos of clouds at all.  These clouds were all different shapes.  There was a lion, a shoal of fish, a whale and a wide oak tree.  They were all beautiful.

At the bottom of the box there was a photograph of a woman with long dark hair, standing beside a big black barn.  She had her arms crossed, and she was leaning against the barn wall.  The sun was in her eyes, and she was laughing at whoever was taking the picture. I flipped it over:

## Ava Laurent – Cloud Artist
## May 1987

I remembered what Grandad had told me on Friday afternoon when I'd said I didn't have time to listen: *"Ava Laurent was the finest cloud sculptor that this country has ever seen."*

I stared at the woman in the photograph and her dark brown eyes twinkled back at me. I thought about the strange black barn with the cabinet full of "carving knives" and the thing moving under the sheeting. Could one of Grandad's silly stories actually be true? Was Ava Laurent an actual cloud sculptor?

"Don't be ridiculous, Tabby," I whispered to myself. And then I quickly put the photographs back in the box and placed the lid down firmly.

# Chapter 8

Mum and Dad said I didn't have to go to Grandad's funeral if I didn't want to. I wasn't sure what to do, and I kept changing my mind. At the last minute I decided I would go, so Mum rang the school to say I wouldn't be in.

The funeral service was really sad and I thought I would cry, but I didn't. In fact, I hadn't cried at all since Grandad died. My chest felt like there was a big balloon filling up the space behind my ribcage. The balloon was being stretched almost to bursting point, but still the tears didn't come.

When the funeral was over, everyone came back to our house for sandwiches, cakes and cups of tea. Mum had placed all our spare chairs in any available space, apart from Grandad's room, which had the door closed.

Dad asked me to take a plate of sandwiches around, and everyone said what a brave girl I was and how Grandad must have been so proud of me. I bit my lip. I didn't think Grandad would have been proud at all. I thought about how I'd always been in a rush to get away from him.

When I went back to the kitchen, I spotted Buster sitting in the corner. He looked scared as he stared up at the strangers' legs around him. I told Mum that I could take Buster for his walk now, and she agreed.

I ran upstairs and changed out of my smart clothes into jeans and a jumper. When I took Buster's lead off the hook by the front door, he spotted me and trotted over.

"Let's get out of here, shall we?" I said, clipping his lead on. Buster smacked his lips together and wagged his tail.

When we got to the pier, the sandy beach on the right was completely empty. School was finished for the day, but the drama department were holding auditions for the next musical production. Rebecca and Lily would definitely be there.

When I'd gone back to school after Grandad had died, Rebecca had come up to me in form and said she was really sorry to hear what had happened. I'd thanked her, and she'd smiled and walked off with Lily. A few seconds later I'd heard them laughing about something.

At the pier Buster stopped to sniff the ground next to the claw machine stuffed with the fluffy frogs. He must have remembered that he'd found a dropped ice cream there.

"Hello again!" said a voice.

It was Alex.  He had a black dog with him.

"How did the funeral go?" Alex asked.
"Actually … that was a ridiculous question.  I'm
sure it was horrible."

I smiled at him.  "It wasn't too bad," I said.
"Not as bad as I thought it was going to be,
anyway."

Buster and the black dog began to sniff each
other's bottoms.

"Is he yours?" I asked.

"Yep!" said Alex, patting the side of the dog.
"This is Dave.  He's a Labrador and a bit deaf, so
we have to shout at him sometimes.  DON'T WE,
DAVE?"

I giggled as the dog ignored Alex and wagged
his tail at Buster, who was going round and
round in circles like an idiot.

"We're going down to the sea if you fancy it?" said Alex.

I shrugged. "OK," I said.

When we got to the pebbly beach, Dave ran straight into the water. Buster watched on, yapping madly at him.

"Dave loves the sea," said Alex. "He always goes in, no matter how cold it is."

I put my hands in my pockets to keep them warm. It was pretty windy, and every now and then I felt a light spray of seawater on my face.

"Dave! DAVE!" shouted Alex, walking towards the shore. Dave was swimming further and further out. His black head bobbed up and down as the waves passed underneath him.

"Dave! YOU'RE GOING THE WRONG WAY!" said Alex. "TURN AROUND!"

I giggled and wondered if Alex would have to wade in to get him. Buster was spinning round, wagging his tail and barking.

Dave suddenly turned and began heading back towards us. His mouth was wide open as he paddled. He looked like he was laughing.

"Come on!" Alex said. "You know you're not allowed to swim out that far."

Dave walked out of the sea and shook himself, showering all of us with cold water.

"Urgh!" I said, laughing.

"Sorry about that," said Alex, smiling at me. We carried on walking.

"Oh look," I said. "The beach huts have been moved."

All the pastel huts were now standing in a row in the field beside the car park. I felt a lump form in my throat when I thought about my chat with Grandad. He'd asked if they'd been moved, ready for the winter. I shook my head, trying to block out the memory. Then I looked up at the strange house perched on the headland.

"Do you know anything about that place?" I said to Alex, pointing towards the dirty white house.

"The House of Clouds?" said Alex. "Just that an artist used to live there or something. The whole place is empty now, I think."

"Do you know why it's called the House of Clouds?" I asked.

I thought about the box of photographs that Grandad had kept on top of his wardrobe and his story about Ava Laurent.

"No," Alex said. "I don't even know if it's a real name or just what some people around here call it."

I remembered the sign I'd found, but I didn't say anything.

We got to the end of the beach and walked up the wooden steps to the promenade. Dave and Buster scampered up behind us and waited while we attached their leads.

We walked along the promenade, then turned towards the car park.

"Grandad said a woman called Ava lived there. Ava Laurent," I said. I didn't want to tell Alex what Grandad had said about her carving clouds into shapes. It sounded too ridiculous.

"Oh, right," said Alex. He waited for a moment while Dave sniffed at a patch of grass. I carried on, but when I got to the track that led to the house I stopped. The wooden sign was still face down on the ground where I'd left it.

The House of Clouds.
An artist who was a sculptor.
The box of photographs of clouds.

This was all beginning to sound a bit … weird. I stared down the track at the house, with its dark windows and peeling paintwork.

"Tabby?" said Alex, catching me up. "Are you OK?"

I nodded and was about to turn away when something caught my attention. In the top right-hand window was a light. I took a few steps along the track and squinted at the window. A shadow fell across the glass and my heart began to hammer. The shadow blocked out the light for a moment, then turned away.

Alex walked over and stood beside me. I turned to face him.

"I think there's someone in there," I said.

# Chapter 9

I began to ramble as I told Alex everything that had happened.

"Before Grandad died, I had a look around the outside of the house," I said. "There's a big barn at the back with some strange stuff inside."

"What kind of stuff?" said Alex.

"There were shelves full of boxes of scientific equipment and this cabinet full of elaborate knives," I said. Alex's eyes widened. "There was also something covered in a sheet, and it looked like it was moving. I don't think the house is abandoned at all. Shall we take a closer look?"

Alex took a deep breath.

"I don't know," he said, staring at the house. "It looks kind of creepy. And I don't like the sound of those knives."

I thought about all the people at our house, dressed in black and drinking tea. I didn't fancy going home yet. And besides, I'd only start looking at my phone and feel bad when I saw more selfies of Rebecca and Lily at the school musical auditions.

I looked back at the glowing orange light in the window. Maybe that shadow belonged to Ava Laurent? The lady in the photograph, whom Grandad had called a "cloud artist".

"Well, I'm going to have a look," I said.

I pulled on Buster's lead and we headed across the long grass. I heard Alex sigh and then the jingle of Dave's lead as they began to follow.

We stood to the side of the house. Dave started to whine.

"Now what do we do?" said Alex.

I didn't get a chance to answer. There was a low creak as the front door began to open. A woman stepped out with her hands on her hips.

"Can I help you?" she said to us.

Dave wagged his tail and pulled Alex towards the door. Buster quickly followed and the two dogs dragged us towards the mysterious woman.

She looked about the same age as Mum, with long brown hair braided into a plait that snaked around the side of her neck. She was wearing a long, white billowy dress, and she had kind eyes and a soft smile on her face – even though her words hadn't been exactly welcoming. She was far too young to be Ava.

"Um, hello," I said. "We were, um ... We were looking for Ava. Ava Laurent?"

The woman's eyes widened when she heard the name, and she blinked a few times.

"I see," she said. "No one has asked for Ava for many years now. And you are?"

"I'm Tabby and this is Alex," I said. "My grandad told me that he knew Ava. We were just ... um ... passing, and I thought I'd see if she was here."

The woman nodded.

"And your grandad is?" she said, folding her arms.

"Was," I said. "He died just last week. George Robert Baker was his name."

Something caught in my throat. I don't know why I included his middle name. I'd only just found out what it was at the funeral.

The woman's eyes widened again.

"Ah, I'm so sorry," she said. "I remember George. You'd better come in."

She turned and went back inside, leaving the door wide open for us to follow.

Alex looked at me and shrugged. I peered inside the hallway. Everything was clean and painted white. It was the complete opposite of how the outside looked.

"Aren't you coming?" the woman called. Her head poked round a door further down the hallway. I looked at Alex, and we both stepped inside.

"Would you both like some lemonade?" the woman asked as we walked into the kitchen.

"Yes, please," I said.

"Oh wow, it's so ... nice," said Alex, looking around. "I wasn't expecting this at all."

The lady smiled.

"Ava liked to keep herself to herself, so it suited her if people thought the house was empty. She could maintain her privacy that way, you see?"

I nodded. The woman had a slight accent. French, I thought.

"And is Ava here?" I asked.

The lady poured some pale lemonade from a jug into two glasses and passed one to me and one to Alex.

"I'm afraid she passed away in a care home about six months ago," she said. "Ava must have lost touch with your grandfather, so I guess he never knew."

"I'm sorry," said Alex.

The lady smiled at him.

"I'm Amelie, Ava's niece," she said. "I've been staying here for a while, sorting out her things."

I stood beside the table, which was scattered with photographs. Amelie came over and began to search through the pictures.

"I've got a photograph here that might be of interest to you, Tabby," Amelie said. I took a sip of my lemonade. It was sharp and sweet at the same time and nothing like the stuff you got in the supermarket. It was delicious.

"Ah, here it is," said Amelie. She smiled as she passed a small square photograph to me. The picture was of a young girl standing on a pebbly beach – the beach that Alex and I had just been walking on. Behind the girl was an older woman and next to her was a man and another lady. They were all grinning at the camera. The man had his hand at his forehead, shielding his eyes from the sun. I looked closely. I recognised the man.

"Is that … my grandad?" I said.

"Yes," said Amelie. "And that little girl at the front is me." She pointed at the photo. "That's my aunt Ava and that's your grandmother. They were all friends."

I stared at the faces laughing back at the camera. They were all so happy. It looked like someone had cracked a joke just before the photo was taken.

"I used to come here in the summer holidays, and I remember your grandparents being really lovely," said Amelie. "Your grandfather definitely had some funny tales to tell!"

I placed the photograph back onto the table. Grandad must have been telling his stories for years, and not just to me. Maybe Amelie knew more?

"My grandad said that Ava was some kind of artist," I said. "Is that true?"

Amelie paused for a moment, then turned away to put the jug of lemonade back in the fridge.

"You could say that, I guess," she said. "Ava was very talented."

Amelie seemed to avoid my eyes. It was like she didn't want to say any more.

"What kind of thing did she do?" said Alex. "Paintings?"

Amelie gave a small smile.

"No, not paintings," she said.

I quickly stepped forwards. "Did she sculpt clouds?" I blurted out.

Alex and Amelie both stared at me.

"I mean ... I know it sounds silly," I went on, "but ... well, my grandad, he used to tell me these stories, and ... well ... I just wondered if ... that one might be true?"

I could feel tears beginning to prickle the back of my eyes like tiny feathers. I looked down at the floor. Buster was asleep by my feet, and his little shoulders rose and fell.

"I'm not sure what your grandfather told you," Amelie said, "but—"

"Forget it," I said quickly, feeling my face turning red. "It's a ridiculous story. Thank you for the drink, but I'd better get home."

I gave Buster a prod with my foot. He jumped up, and I turned and walked down the hallway and out of the wide front door.

What was I thinking? I couldn't believe I had said it out loud. I couldn't believe that for one second I had actually thought that Grandad's story about a woman who sculpts clouds might have been true.

Alex caught me up just as I got across the car park.

"What was that all about?" he said. "What did you mean, sculpting clouds?"

There was a bit of amusement in Alex's voice. Dave and Buster trotted beside each other like they'd been friends for years. I pulled Buster back a bit.

"Just forget it," I said.

Alex ran in front of me, blocking my way.

"I'm not laughing at you, Tabby," he said. "I just wanted to know what it was that your grandad told you."

I exhaled.

"My grandad loved to tell me stories," I said. "When I was little, I really enjoyed them. But the thing is, he never stopped. He kept telling me stupid things that were clearly made up. Like his story about a ship in a bottle! He loved that one. He told me countless times that it had been made by bumble bees."

Alex smiled.

"But then Grandad told me about an artist called Ava Laurent who lived in the House of Clouds. He said that she pulled clouds down from the sky, carved them into shapes and then released them for everyone to enjoy. He said ... he said that artists like Ava were becoming extinct because no one looks up any more. And ... and I just wished that one of his stories was true."

Alex smiled at me.

"I think that's a wonderful story," he said.

"But that's just it, isn't it?" I said. "It's a story. It's made up."

I felt a tear roll down my cheek, and I wiped it away.

"I wish I'd listened to him more, Alex," I said. "I wish I'd just given him more time. And now he's gone, and there's nothing I can do about it."

Alex was quiet for a moment.

"I'm so sorry, Tabby," he said.

"Thanks for the walk," I said. "I'll see you at school on Monday."

I quickly walked away and headed home.

# Chapter 10

The next morning, I woke up and checked my phone.  There was a photograph of Lily looking really bored in the back of a car on her way to visit family in Wales.  At least I wouldn't be bombarded with photos of her and Rebecca out doing fun things all weekend.

I could hear Mum and Dad sorting out Grandad's room.  When I went downstairs, his bed had gone and our dining table had returned from the garage and been put back where it used to be.  I wished Grandad's bed was there instead.

"Tabby, I know you might not want to think about it right now," Mum said, "but is there

anything of Grandad's that you'd like to have?
We don't have room to keep everything, but I
thought it would be nice if you wanted to choose
something special."

Straight away I looked up at the shelf and
at Grandad's ship in a bottle. I walked over and
carefully lifted it up.

"Can I have this?" I said. "I promise I'll look
after it."

Mum smiled at me.

"Of course you can," she said. "He'd be so pleased you chose it."

I took the bottle upstairs and sat cross-legged on my bed. I wiped the glass and stared in at the ship. It really was a fascinating object. I was just wondering if it had been modelled on a real ship when my phone began to ring. It was Alex.

"Hello?" I said.

"Tabby! Are you free? Can you meet me at the pier in ten minutes?" Alex sounded out of breath.

"I ... um ... yeah, I guess," I said, staring down at my pyjamas.

"Great!" said Alex. "And bring Buster!"

The phone went dead. I sat there for a second, and then I got up and grabbed my clothes.

Five minutes later, I headed to the pier, Buster trotting along beside me. I normally took him for walks later in the day, and he seemed really happy that we were going out early for once. When he spotted Dave, he began to pull on his lead.

"Hold up, Buster," I said. "No rush!"

"Tabby! Quick, follow me," said Alex. "She said we've got to be sitting on the sea wall in exactly five minutes."

Alex ushered me towards the pebbly beach.

"Who said that?" I asked. "What's going on?"

Dave and Buster began to jump around and bark as if they could sense Alex's excitement.

He grinned at me. "It's a surprise!" Alex said. He checked his watch. "Come on. There's only a few minutes to go!"

We walked around the pier to the promenade, and Alex let Dave off his lead. I let Buster go as well. The two dogs ran across the pebbles, and Dave splashed straight into the sea.

"OK," Alex said. "I think if we sit about here, then we'll have the best view."

He sat down on the sea wall, swung his legs around and patted the space beside him. "Sit here and wait," Alex said, smiling.

I frowned at him, then sat down. The wall was cold against my legs, but I could still feel the heat from the sun on my face. It was probably the last warmth before winter took charge of the weather.

"I don't get it," I said. "What are we waiting for?"

Alex looked behind us and then back at me.

"We're waiting for this," he said, pointing to the bright blue sky.

I twisted around to see what Alex was pointing at.

A cloud appeared over our heads. It had a long part at the front and a wide, bulbous middle. I stared at the cloud's sweeping curves and the different shades of white and grey that merged in the middle. And then I realised what the cloud was.

"It's a ship in a bottle!" I said.

I quickly fumbled to my feet and stood on the sea wall in the bright sunshine. The cloud floated right over our heads. I could make out the billowing sails of the ship inside the wispy white shape of the bottle. The ship looked like it was just setting off on a trip across the ocean to lands far away.

I felt tears stream down my face as I watched the sculpted cloud drift further and further away.

"Your grandad was telling the truth after all, Tabby," said Alex. "Yesterday I went back to the house and spoke to Amelie. I told her everything that you'd said: about the cloud sculptor, how your grandad had made up a story about his ship in a bottle. Amelie listened and told me to bring you back here this morning at nine and to watch the sky. Amelie must be a cloud sculptor as well!"

I grinned at Alex, and then I turned back, just as a gentle breeze carried the cloud further away. The ship in a bottle twisted slightly, and before long it wasn't a bottle at all. It was just a cloud, floating out to sea.

My face was wet with tears, and I wiped my cheeks with my sleeves.

"Goodbye, Grandad," I whispered. "Have a good trip."

# Chapter 11

After the ship in a bottle had faded into the bright blue sky, Alex and I headed towards the House of Clouds. I couldn't speak. I felt as if I was floating like a cloud myself. It was true! Grandad's story was true!

A black jeep appeared at the end of the track to the house, and its window wound down. Amelie was in the driver's seat. She lifted up her sunglasses and placed them on the top of her head.

"I was hoping I'd see you," she said.

"That was amazing!" I said. "That cloud looked *exactly* like Grandad's ship in a bottle. Are you a cloud artist too? Just like Ava? How do you carve them? Can you show us how you do it?"

Amelie smiled but didn't answer my questions. "I need to get to the airport now, Tabby, but I'll be back," she said. "Here. This is for you." Amelie reached down for something in the side of her door and passed it through the window. It was an envelope.

I clutched the envelope to my chest as she put her sunglasses back on.

"Bye, Tabby, bye, Alex," Amelie said, and the black jeep slowly drove away.

"Why is she going?" I said. "I've got so many questions!"

"She said she'd be back," said Alex. "Maybe you can ask her next time?"

I held up the envelope. On the front it read *For Tabby* in elegant handwriting. I opened it. Inside was a photograph: the photo of Amelie, Ava and my grandparents standing on the beach. I looked again at their smiling faces and then turned the photograph over. Something was written on the back.

"*There is wonder all around you, Tabby,*" I read out loud. "*You've just got to remember to look up. From Amelie.*"

I turned to Alex, who was smiling at me, and then I put the photo safely into the envelope. I would keep it in my bedroom and put it right next to the ship in a bottle.

We headed slowly across the car park, and my phone pinged. It was a message from Rebecca:

Hi Tabby.  How are you doing?  I'm
sorry I haven't been in touch since your
grandad died.  Do you fancy coming into
town?  Just the two of us?  x

I smiled to myself, remembering that Lily was in
Wales.  I typed a reply:

Sorry, Rebecca, but I'm busy today.  Have
a nice weekend! x

I hit send, and then I deleted the app that I kept
looking at with all the photos of Rebecca and
Lily having a good time.  As soon as the app
vanished from my screen, I felt a great sense of
relief.  Why hadn't I done that sooner?

"Oh yeah, I forgot to tell you," said Alex.  "I
found some of that shampoo for Buster that I
told you about.  For his skin condition?  I could
help you give him a bath if you like?"

Alex seemed shy for a moment. Like he was embarrassed to be offering to help. Buster did a little spin in front of us as Dave wiggled his bottom beside him. They were so funny together.

"Sure," I said, laughing as the dogs bounded around us. "That'll be great."

Our books are tested
for children and young people by
children and young people.

Thanks to everyone who consulted on
a manuscript for their time and effort in
helping us to make our books better
for our readers.